Baffle That Bully!

The game that puts YOU in control and makes the bully lose interest

(aka: how to totally confuse – and finally get rid of – your bully!)

By Chase Anichini & Amy Jones Anichini

Illustrated by Jordan Anichini & Chase Anichini

BaffleThatBully.com

To the people who have been struggling with bullies for a really long time and really want to get rid of them --- CA

To my husband Tom for his support and encouragement and for empowering our daughters by teaching them the distraction techniques that inspired this book --- AJA

TABLE of CONTENTS

Preface: What My Parents Want Your Parents To Know

OK, so let's begin our relationship with complete honesty: I moved a bunch of the stuff my mom wrote for this section to the back of the book. It's alright for me to do that, because this is my book!

Truth is, I thought it was kind of . . . . **D U L L** . . . . and I didn't want you to get bored and stop reading before I taught you my cool game.

Here's a summary of what she wrote to your parents:

1. This Book Deals More with Emotional & Verbal Bullying Rather than Physical Bullying

2. Please Read This Book With Your Child and Help Them Prepare to Play the Game

3. Scarlett Jones is Not a Real Person

4. Bullying Does Happen in Elementary School

So, if you're a parent, please flip to Page 54 in the BACK of the book (if you want to) so you can read what my parents would like for you to know.

If you're a kid, then head over to the next page, and let's get started!

Nice To Meet You!

Hi! I'm Scarlett, and I'm in 3rd grade. My favorite subject is science; it's so cool! I also like to read. In fact, sometimes after my mom puts me to bed, I sneak into the bathroom, close the door, sit on the floor and read with the flashlight for hours! Shhh - don't tell.

Also, I'm really good at math, but I can't stand that subject.

What I really like is recess! I get to run around with my friend Caroline. We act all crazy, put on pretend talent shows, do gymnastics, and swing on the monkey bars. My mom told me to take a break from the monkey bars, because my hands keep getting blisters which never heal, because I pick at them. How can I NOT pick at them? They're there, aren't they? Anyway, I agreed to take a break from the monkey bars so my hands could heal, and so I wouldn't complain when I had to do my homework, because the blisters hurt when I hold my pencil.

So I took a break for one day. That should do it, right?

Know what else I like?

- ♥ Shoes ♥
- ♥ And lip gloss ♥
- ♥ And nail polish ♥
- ♥ And doing a different hairstyle every day with NO assistance, thank you very much ♥

So, you see: I'm just a regular kid like you.

If you're reading this, I bet we have something in common. And it's good for us to talk about this, because you need to know that you're not the only kid with this problem. Know what else? It's not your fault, and it can happen to anybody. After all, we didn't ask for this. Know what I'm talking about?

OK, I'll just say it: I was bullied.

There. It's out. I feel better. Do you?

Hum, OK maybe I'm getting ahead of myself. I do that when I get excited! You might not feel better yet but you will - trust me. Wanna know why? Because I'm going to teach you how I got rid of my bullies.

And then you're going to get rid of yours.

Wanna know what the best part is? It's a game! I call it, "Baffle that Bully!"

Good vocab word, right? Do you know what "baffle" means? If you do, cool. If not, be sure to tell your teacher you learned a new word.

Baffle: To totally bewilder or perplex; to defeat by confusing or puzzling

I know what you're thinking: "What the heck do bewilder and perplex mean?"

By the way, did you see what I just did there? Whenever I think I hear you asking me something, I'll put it in yellow highlighter, OK?

Bewilder: To cause someone to lose their bearings

Perplex: To confuse someone with uncertainty or doubt

"Wow, that's a lot of information!"

I know. But, really, all you need to remember is that I am going to show you how to totally confuse (and finally get rid of!) your bully.

Now, doesn't it sound like this might even possibly be just a tiny little bit ... fun?

To tell you the truth, that's kind of the point: to turn things around and start being the one who's having fun.

Right now, they seem to be having fun picking on you, don't they? They think they look cool around their friends, right?

Well, what if it wasn't fun for them anymore? There wouldn't be much of a reason to pick on you anymore, would there? So guess what you and I are going to do? We're going to take away their fun.

Are you ready? Let's go:

Game Rules, Goal, & How To Play

First, as with any game, there are rules.

The (Kind of Boring but You've Got to Learn Them Anyway) Rules:

1. Do not be mean

2. Do not have a nasty tone in your voice

3. Remain calm – I know, that one's easier said than done, but we'll work on that

4. Don't sink to their level – in other words, don't bully the bullies

5. Treat them and everyone else the way you want to be treated

6. Prepare your responses ahead of time

7. Don't let them change how you feel about yourself

8. Always remember that you are an amazing kid who deserves to be happy and to live your life in peace

And, of course, we have a goal.

The Very Important Goal:

To get the bullies to decide for themselves to leave you alone, because it's no longer fun for them to torment you.

How to Play:

<u>Step #1</u>:   Do not react to what they say or do: Stomach Breathe

<u>Step #2</u>:   Smile by thinking Happy Thoughts

<u>Step #3</u>:   Say or do something Completely Random & Harmless that is unrelated to what they said or did to you

OK, now, I can hear what you're saying:

"Scarlett, how can I NOT react when they are saying all these mean things about me that aren't true?!"

OR

"They have made me so _____ (fill in the blank: sad, mad, upset, exhausted, depressed, etc.) that I have NOTHING to smile about."

OR

"You want me to say something to them? I am NOT talking to those jerks. Everybody says to just ignore them."

But, humor me for just a minute here: is any of what you're doing right now helping you get rid of your bullies???

No ...

Yep, I know. That stuff didn't work for me either. So let me teach you more about the 3 Steps to Playing Baffle that Bully.

More Info About How to Play Baffle That Bully: The 3 Steps

How To Play the Game

Step #1: Do Not React To What They Say or Do: Stomach Breathe

Have you ever seen one of those "Peanuts" cartoons that our parents used to watch when they were kids? You know, the ones with Charlie Brown and Snoopy? Whenever the teacher or the parents talk, this is what the Peanuts kids hear:

WAA WU WAA WAA WAAA. WU WA WAA WA WAA...

That's what I want you to repeat over and over in your head when the bullies are talking.

When you pretend like their words are garbledy gook, it makes it easier to not react. Besides, what they say doesn't matter, because they don't really know the real you.

"Scarlett, this is never going to work. I just get so nervous and upset when they bother me. My heart starts racing, I feel kinda sweaty, and my hands even shake!"

Me, too. That's where stomach breathing comes in handy.

I know, I know: "What the heck is stomach breathing?"

You know how when you're upset or nervous, people are always telling you to take a deep breath? OK, well, what they really mean is

"Stomach Breathe"

Let your stomach move in and out while you breathe. This is different from "chest breathing" where your chest goes in and out when you breathe:

Chest Breathing Can Make You Kind Of Hyper!!!!

When you **Stomach Breathe**, it helps you calm down. Staying calm is key to not reacting to a bully.

Try this: put your hand on your stomach. Now, let your stomach totally relax. Next, take a deep breath in and while you do, allow your stomach to move out, kind of like you're making room in your tummy for all of that air. When you breathe out, let your stomach go in like it's a balloon deflating. So:

Breathe in => Stomach out
Breathe out => Stomach in

I know it sounds totally crazy. But there is something about moving your stomach when you breathe (instead of moving your chest) that is relaxing.

Tonight, when you're going to sleep, try it, and see how quickly you fall asleep.

Whenever you feel yourself starting to react to the bullies, take a quick second to make sure you are **Stomach Breathing**. Then you'll be calm no matter what they do. And, if you're busy focusing on your breathing to make sure you're doing it the "calming" way, you won't really have time to think about whether or not they just said something mean to you.

How To Play the Game
Step #2: Smile by Thinking "Happy Thoughts"

To do this, all you have to do is think about what makes you happy **("Happy Thoughts")**, and then just smile. How about if we come up with a list? I love doing this, so I'm going to go a little crazy here listing mine:

Scarlett's Happy Thoughts:

 Puppies

 Kittens

 Summertime

 Orange Fanta

Ice cream

 A day at the beach

 Swimming in my neighbor's pool

 Laying on the grass and looking up at the clouds

 Snow

 My favorite outfit

 TV

 My favorite song

You know, I could just go on and on and on ...

How about you? Go get some paper and a pencil, and write down your **Happy Thoughts.**

Now, every night, before you go to bed, read over your list or just think about it while you're going to sleep. Then you'll have all of these wonderful **Happy Thoughts** fresh in your mind for when you need to smile around a bully.

Come up with some places in your house where you can post your **Happy**

Thoughts so they can cheer you up anytime. I like to tape my list to the back of my bedroom door so I can read it every time I leave my room. You could also post your list near the door you use when you're leaving your house. That way you can read them over before you head out the door!

Where do you think you might post your list? Write down some ideas in the back of the book or on a separate sheet of paper.

The great thing is this: if you're trying to smile by thinking about your **Happy Thoughts**, you'll be focused more on the **Happy Thoughts** than on what the bully just said or did. This will make it very difficult for the bully to upset you!

How To Play the Game

Step #3: Say or do Something "Completely Random & Harmless"

Actually, I named Step #3:

"Say or Do Something Completely Random & Harmless That is Unrelated to What They Just Said or Did to You"

But I couldn't fit that long title in the cloud up there! So, to keep things simple, I am going to call all of this stuff:

"Completely Random & Harmless Comments"

Now, your **Completely Random & Harmless Comments** can really be anything at all. The sky is the limit, EXCEPT:

a. It must have nothing to do with what they just said or did

b. It must be harmless

For example, you can **make a harmless comment** about them, such as:

 Nice shirt.

 Cool shoes.

 I like your earrings.

Or you can **ask them a harmless question,** like:

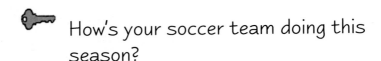 How's your soccer team doing this season?

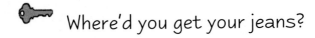 Where'd you get your jeans?

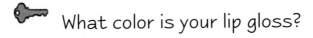 What color is your lip gloss?

 Did you just get a haircut?

Or you can <u>__say something completely__</u> <u>__random__</u>, like:

- I hate broccoli.
- There's going to be an eclipse tonight.

Or you can <u>__ask a completely random__</u> <u>__question__</u> like:

- Is it supposed to rain tomorrow?
- What's the first day of school next year?
- How much does a dog cost?

Or you can <u>use one of my personal favorites</u>:

- You can simply smile your most genuine smile!
- You can laugh like you're having the time of your life!

"But, Scarlett, I can't say that stuff to them; they'll pick on me even more! They are going to think I'm even MORE strange! "

To which my responses are:

1st: Who cares what they think?

2nd: You don't know what they'll do until you try something different.

3rd: The correct response to the statement, "You're weird!" or "You're strange!" is ALWAYS:

"Thank you!"

(with that same smile from Step #2 on your face)

Listen, I'm not going to lie to you. It might take a while to get rid of your bullies. You might get discouraged, and you'll probably feel strange playing this game. But if you play this game correctly, your bully will eventually be so confused ("baffled") by your behavior that he or she will leave you alone. It will absolutely not be fun for him or her anymore!

The key to Step #3 is to come up with a list of **Completely Random & Harmless Comments** that YOU are comfortable with. If you like some of mine, use them! If you can't see yourself saying some of the same things as me, then come up with your very own list. Brainstorm (maybe even ask your parents what they think), and write them down just like you did with your **Happy Thoughts**. Then, look over them every day so they are fresh in your mind for when you need them.

How about if I tell you about some of my real experiences, so you can get a better idea of how this works? These situations used to be awful for me, but wait until you see how the bullies reacted when I refused to play their game and instead decided to baffle them!

The Bully Encounters
of
Scarlett the Baffler!

Scarlett the Baffler!

Bully Makes Fun of My Name

Bully Robert: Hey, Jones, you got weak bones. I'm gonna hit you with some stones.

Time to play Baffle That Bully!

Me: 1. Don't react: Stomach Breathe

2. Smile

3. I say harmlessly,

"Nice shirt, Robert."

(Remember Step 3 is my **Completely Random & Harmless Comment**, so my tone is genuine: I really do like his shirt! There is no hidden message here.)

Bully Robert: What? What? Why are you talking about my shirt? What's wrong with my shirt?

Robert is a little concerned about his shirt, even though I didn't say anything hurtful or mean. Maybe he's ... (hum, what's the word I'm looking for here?) Oh, I know: BAFFLED! I took the fun out of picking on me, and he left me alone, which was exactly what I wanted.

Scarlett the Baffler!
BULLIES TRY TO
SCARE ME

BULLY BRUCE: WHY ARE YOU DRAWING A DUCK WHEN THE ASSIGNMENT WAS TO DRAW ABOUT SOMETHING YOU'RE DOING RIGHT NOW?

Me: I'm in a play right now, and I'm playing a duckling.

BULLY BRUCE: HEY, ROBERT. SCARLETT'S A HELPLESS LITTLE DUCKY! ISN'T IT DUCK SEASON? GET YOUR GUN!

Bully Robert: Yeah, let's shoot her down.

Then they both pretend to be holding guns pointed at me and start making shooting sounds.

Time to play Baffle That Bully!

Me: 1. Don't react: Stomach Breathe

2. Smile

3. I say harmlessly,

"Bruce, I've been meaning to ask you how baseball season's going."

BULLY BRUCE: WHAT? WHY ARE YOU ... WHAT ARE YOU ASKING ME ABOUT BASEBALL FOR? WE'RE NOT TALKING ABOUT BASEBALL, YOU WEIRDO.

Me: (Still playing Baffle That Bully!)

1. Still not reacting; still <u>Stomach Breathing</u>

2. Still smiling

3. I shrug and say harmlessly,

"Just wondering."

Bruce rolled his eyes and walked off. I took the fun out of it for him. Robert got really quiet – guess he was baffled … again!

Teeheehee!

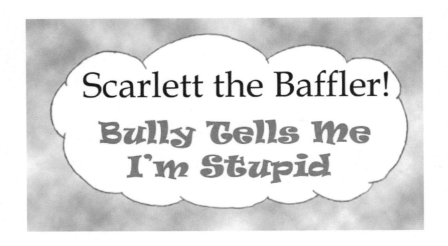

Scarlett the Baffler!

Bully Tells Me I'm Stupid

Bully Daisy is on her way back to her desk after sharpening her pencil. When she passes my desk, she whispers in my ear, "Stupid."

I know that YOU know that bullies are very clever about doing things so no one else notices. Daisy doesn't want the teacher to catch her, so she doesn't even look at me until she's back sitting down at her desk. Of course, she's dying to see my reaction and really wants to know that she's made me feel bad.

There really is only one way to handle this type of encounter. I wait until she's back at her desk and is looking at me to make sure I'm upset. Then:

Time to play Baffle That Bully!

1. Don't react: Stomach Breathe
2. Smile my biggest, happiest smile (I'm thinking of one of my **Happy Thoughts**.)

Then Daisy does what I call the "caveman face": she scrunches her eyebrows down so they look like they are built right onto her eyelids AND she gets her mouth in an under bite so that all I can see is her lower teeth. Her look says,

"You're not supposed to be happy (grumble, grumble, grumble...)"

What did I do? I just kept smiling!

Scarlett the Baffler!

BULLY MIMICS ME

Me: Mrs. Smith, did you say to stop at the bottom of page 32 or page 33?

Bully Sam, who sits next to me and thinks he and Bruce are long-lost twins, gets a very annoying whiny tone in his voice and repeats everything I say, so I can hear him but the teacher can't.

BULLY SAM: *Mrs. Smith, did you say to stop at the bottom of page 32 or page 33?*

Time to play Baffle That Bully!

Me: 1. Don't react: <u>Stomach Breathe</u>

2. (Smiling on the inside) I get a very sympathetic look on my face

3. I say harmlessly,

"Oh, my goodness, Sam. Are you OK? Your voice just got so high – oh, no! Do you need to go to the nurse's office? Gosh, this could be serious; hang on, and I'll ask the teacher for the nurse's pass."

My voice is filled with genuine concern, because why else would he sound so strange? He must really be sick…

BULLY SAM: WHAT? I'M NOT SICK ...
YOU'RE SICK! YOU'RE SICK! YOU'RE ...
WHATEVER!

Still playing Baffle That Bully!

Me: 1. Don't react: <u>Stomach Breathe</u>

2. Smile

3. I say harmlessly,

"I'm just fine, thanks."

Scarlett the Baffler!
BULLIES TRY TO MAKE ME HOPELESS & ALL ALONE

The teacher told us to talk to our table group about what we did over the winter break. Unfortunately for me, at this time, my table group was me and 3 boys who, over the course of a few months, gradually joined together to bully me.

Me: Well, we went to Chicago, which was really awesome, because all of my cousins ...

BULLY OLIVER: WHY ARE YOU TALKING? SHUT UP.

BULLY SAM: YEAH, WHY DON'T YOU JUST STOP TALKING? NOBODY CARES WHAT YOU THINK.

BULLY BRUCE: NOBODY CARES ABOUT YOU OR YOUR FAMILY.

(OK, hit pause)

This was as bad as it got for me. I really really really really wanted to cry. I wanted to crawl in a hole and never come out again ... ever. I wanted to quit school and never leave my house again.

BUT, I was playing Baffle that Bully, and I was going to win. So, there was really only one response that could work:

Time to play Baffle That Bully!

Me: 1. Don't react: Stomach Breathe

2. Smile

3. I start dying laughing! I imagine the cutest puppy in the world jumping into my

lap and licking my face. I imagine my sweet, tiny baby sister letting out the biggest burp I've ever heard. I imagine Oliver, Sam, and Bruce in fancy dresses, high heels, nail polish, and lip gloss. I laugh and laugh and laugh.

BULLY OLIVER: WHY ARE YOU LAUGHING? THIS ISN'T FUNNY. YOU'RE NOT SUPPOSED TO LAUGH!

BULLY SAM: YEAH, YOU'RE NOT SUPPOSED TO BE LAUGHING. YOU'RE WEIRD!

Still playing Baffle That Bully!

Me: 1. Don't react: Stomach Breathe

2. Smile

3. I say harmlessly,

"Thank you."

Because the only response to someone who says you are weird or strange or different is:

"Thank you."

Later that day I told my parents what happened. My mom contacted the teacher, who told the principal, who spoke to the boys and then sent them home for the day. Apparently, I wasn't the only one having trouble with those bullies.

Sometimes, you have to get the grown-ups involved.

Here's another thing I want to share with you about how I handled this encounter: I used my thoughts to take away these boys' "power" over me. By dressing them up, it became hard for me to see them as threatening, even though they wanted me to be sad and scared of them. Check it out:

Don't seem so powerful anymore, do they?!

Scarlett's Take on Feelings

Feelings are a funny thing, you know. We mention them a lot, such as:

- So and so hurt my feelings.

- You're a meany — stop hurting my feelings!

- You are making me sad.

- You made me cry.

But we don't really TALK about feelings. And I'm not going to get all touchy/feely here, but there's something I want you to think about with regard to feelings:

Your feelings are yours. They come from your mind. No one can jump into your mind and MAKE you feel a certain way. You are the only one who gets to decide how you feel.

"But, Scarlett, you don't understand! These kids … they are just so mean and cruel and rude. They tell me over and over how everyone hates me. It's so painful to hear those things that it does hurt my feelings."

Well, let me ask you this, "Are they right? Does everyone hate you? I mean every single person on the face of the earth? Do ALL of them really hate you?"

Absolutely not.

So why allow yourself to feel sad about something that's not even true?

Listen, I know it is painful to hear someone say cruel things about you. People really should not treat others that way. You and I are never going to be mean to another person, are we?

How nice would it be if we could control what other people say to us to make sure they only say kind and truthful things? I'd like to live in a world like that! But, unfortunately:

We simply can't control what comes out of other people's mouths. However, we can control how we FEEL about what they say.

Other kids might want to hurt you. They might want to "make you" feel bad. But you know what? They don't get to decide when you feel bad. Only you get to decide that.

No one can make you feel bad unless you allow yourself to feel bad.

So when that "bad or sad" feeling starts showing up, remind yourself that you're in charge of your thoughts and feelings. **Stomach Breathe** to calm down, get those **Happy Thoughts** in your head and remind yourself of all the great things in your life.

It all boils down to this:

The minute you start believing that happiness is a decision, your life will start getting better!

Well, I guess that about wraps it up. Now, take a couple deep **Stomach Breaths**. And remember:

✓ **You can do this!**

✓ **You are not alone.**

✓ **Believe in yourself, because I do.**

Now, go make your list of **Happy Thoughts** and your list of **Completely Random & Harmless Comments**. Then you'll be ready to play the game and ...

Baffle YOUR Bully!

Believe in yourself

Victory!

Self-Confidence

Make it a game

Choose to be happy

Self-Esteem

Don't let anyone bring you down, no matter how hard they try!

Preface:
(Which I Moved to Back Here!)

Remember how I moved this to the end of the book, because I was afraid you might get bored hearing from my Mom first rather than from me? Well, now here it is:

What My Parents Want Your Parents to Know:

1. This Book Deals More with Emotional & Verbal Bullying Rather than Physical Bullying

This book can help teach your child how to handle many situations where someone says something that "hurts their feelings." These unpleasant encounters can be as innocuous as when two best friends are not getting along and one says something hurtful to the other. Or they can be as severe as dealing with a bully who constantly picks on or belittles your child.

We present tools to help children deal with (at the extreme end) those kids who pester them, pick on them, call them names, spread rumors about them, or otherwise make their life miserable. This behavior is commonly known as emotional bullying.

Please be aware that we are not addressing physical bullying in this book. If someone is hurting your child physically, we strongly advise you to report the incidents to the teacher, coach, principal, or other appropriate authority figure and consider seeking professional advice.

Our hope is that, while teaching your child how to Baffle That Bully, he/she will not only distract the bully from their well-rehearsed tactics but will also gain confidence. That self-confidence and sense of self-esteem could help your child handle just about any unpleasant situation.

2. Please Read This Book With Your Child and Help Them Prepare to Play the Game

This book was written by a family to help other families. Author Chase Anichini is an elementary school student, and illustrator Jordan Anichini is a middle school student. Author Amy Jones Anichini (that's me) is their mother. While we would not have chosen to have our lives impacted by bullying, dealing with bullying actually brought our family closer together. Nearly 2 years after the bullying started, we decided to share our story with you.

Please read this book with your child. We encourage you to help him/her brainstorm about what makes them happy **(Happy Thoughts)** as well as help them come up with their list of **Completely Random & Harmless Comments** . Having our family exposed to bullying reminded us of just how important it is to not just talk to our children but to really hear them. Sitting down together and talking about our child's painful encounters was one of the keys to helping re-build our daughter's confidence. She was reminded that she does matter in spite of what the bullies might tell her.

Also, practice **Stomach Breathing** together. It's a wonderful way to relax at the end of a long day.

3. Scarlett Jones is Not a Real Person

"Scarlett Jones" is the character our daughter created to help her share her story with you and your child. Because this is such a sensitive subject to discuss, changing her name made it feel like she was talking about a character rather than her real life.

Every situation we present in this book is based on an encounter that actually happened. However, we altered some of the details to protect the identities of the children involved. We changed all of the names and the physical depictions of the children.

Additionally, we altered the settings; we chose to set each situation in the classroom environment because most children who will read this book have experience in a classroom.

Any similarities between the characters in this book and people who our daughter has encountered are unintentional and purely coincidental.

4. Bullying Does Happen in Elementary School

As parents, none of us want to believe that children as young as age 7 can bully other children. But please do not kid yourself – it does happen. It happened to our daughter, and if you're reading this book, you must at least suspect that it is happening to your child. Living in denial or disbelief will only delay you helping your child solve this problem.

Having said that, based on our daughter's experience we strongly believe that **without a reaction from the target (victim), emotional bullying can't launch. The bully needs a reaction from the target to prompt them to continue bullying.**

So, in a perfect world, we would have a crystal ball that would tell us which unpleasant encounters are one-time incidents and which are the first of what will become multiple miserable experiences that we will ultimately end up calling "bullying." Then, we could advise our children simply not to react to the would-be bullies so that the cycle never starts.

Unfortunately, life is not quite that simple. Often we can't identify a bully or bullying behavior until it has been going on for a long time, which, of course, is what defines bullying. Once your child reacts to something unkind or unfair that a bully says, that might be all that's needed to make the bully think it's fun to pick on your child. Then every time they react to the bully's behavior, the pattern gets more worn and developed, and it becomes more difficult to break the cycle.

But, they must break the cycle. And we think we can help: that's what "Baffle That Bully" is all about.

--- Amy Jones Anichini

Parents: Please visit us online at BaffleThatBully.com where co-authors Amy and Chase as well as heroine Scarlett blog about current topics related to overcoming bullying, refusing to be a victim of bullying, building your confidence, creating your own happiness, and the power of positive thinking. You and your child/tween can even ask Scarlett a question, and she'll help them!

Learn more @ **bafflethatbully.com**

Would you like to talk to Scarlett? You can! bafflethatbully.com/ask-scarlett/

Made in the USA
Monee, IL
22 October 2022